Cooper and Me™

and the Winter Adventure!

Written by Monique & Alexa Peters

Illustrated by Alexa Peters & Melissa Peterson

Copyright © 2010 by Monique Peters
Second Edition 2011
ISBN hardcover: 978-0-9829418-3-6
Library of Congress Control Number: 20009813643

Education Advisory Committee
Our advisors review each book in the *Cooper and Me* series
and have earned degrees from these universities, among others:
Ann Beasley, B.S. from St. John's University
Karen Lunny, M.A. from George Mason University
Carolyn Olivier, M.Ed. from Harvard Graduate School of Education

To order additional copies of this book, or other books in this series:
www.CooperandMe.com

Cooper and Me books
are proudly printed in the
U.S.A.

In fond memory of Marc Lustgarten, we dedicate this book. To honor him, we will donate a portion of the net proceeds of this book to the Lustgarten Foundation. Go to www.lustgarten.org for ways to get involved, support, or donate to the cause.

Cooper and Me thanks Nathaniel Ledwith for his literary expertise.

There's a buzz in the air!
There are lights everywhere!

It must be the season
to love and to share!

1

We share all our hugs,
we share gifts by the fire,
we share songs that are sung
by the neighborhood choir.

For Cooper and Bella, it's time to share fun!
They could both build a snowman
that blocks out the sun!

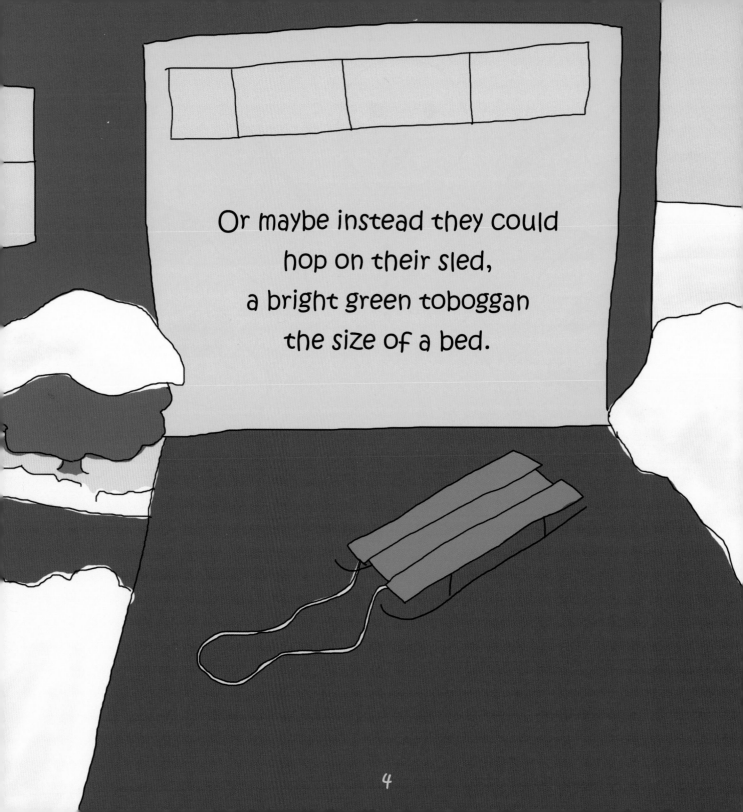

Or maybe instead they could
hop on their sled,
a bright green toboggan
the size of a bed.

"Sledding sounds great!" said both pups aloud,

as they walked past a snowbank that looked like a cloud.

They could glide, slip and slide right over the snow.

There wouldn't be anywhere they couldn't go!

So they got out their sled,
prepared for the chill,
and headed way out
to the town's biggest hill.

7

When they got to the hill,
it started to snow,
so they put on their goggles and gave it a go.

8

They flew past the people.
They swerved around trees.
They skidded over streams
that had started to freeze!

When they got to the bottom, they both looked around.

The whole world was white from the sky to the ground!

Even the air around them was white; it was snowing so much that it blinded their sight!

They wandered a bit, sled always in tow,

but the big piles of snow just continued to grow.

Cooper said,

"Stop! We should stay here and wait."

So they sat there and talked,

but it began to grow late....

Bella said, "Coop, we should both try to bark;

we need to get home before it gets dark!"

They both let out howls, as loud as they could,

and the echoes bounced through

the whole neighborhood.

They waited a moment, both straining to hear

the sound of an answer from far or from near.

17

And then came the barks, as clear as a bell!

"They came from close by!

I'm sure, I can tell!"

So off went the pair, through the snow, cold and wet,
racing to get home before the sun set.
They followed the barks, which got louder and louder,
till the town reappeared through the thick white powder.

"We did it!" grinned Cooper, "We're home at last!"
He was glad any trouble had finally passed.
"But who answered our howls to get us here?
I can still hear him barking. He's got to be near."

It was Trooper, their friend
who was out on a walk,
and he was on his way over,
looking to talk.

21

"Thank you," said Bella. "You saved our whole night!
Being out in that storm gave me kind of a fright."
"Yeah," agreed Cooper, "I was blind as a bat.
I couldn't have gotten home without that!"

22

No problem," said Trooper, "I was looking for you. Anyway, it was the right thing to do."

Information About ME!

My Name

My first name is _____.

My last name is _____.

My Address

I live at _____,

In the town of _____,

In the state of _____.

My phone number is _____.

The People Who Take Care of Me
These are the people who are responsible for taking care of me
and should be contacted to help get me home.

Name: _____

Relationship: _____

Phone number: _____

Name: _____

Relationship: _____

Phone number: _____

For more information and helpful guidelines, contact your local police station.

and the Winter Adventure!

Life Lesson
Being Prepared and Safe in Case You Get Lost

Getting separated from someone you love can be scary when you don't know what to do. Sometimes when you are playing with your friends, or if you are bored, you come up with ideas of activities that seem really fun. Often, you take that adventure or try that activity, not thinking of anything except how exciting it will be. At times, these adventures may be scary or dangerous. If you don't tell a loved one what you are doing, especially when it is something new to you, you could get hurt, lost, or scared. It is important to know what to do when you get separated or lost from your loved ones. You should make sure you are prepared and aware so you can always be safe.

Connections

🐾 How did Cooper and Bella feel when they realized they were lost? Have you ever felt this way?

🐾 What would you do if you were lost? What did Cooper and Bella do?

🐾 What do you think Cooper and Bella will do the next time they are sledding?

Cooper and Me™
and the Winter Adventure!

Learning Together

🐾 **Which season is this book in: summer, fall, winter, or spring?**
This book takes place in the winter season.

🐾 **What is the weather like during this season?**
Winter is the coldest of all the seasons.

🐾 **Who does Cooper play with in the snow?**
Cooper plays with Bella in the snow.

🐾 **What kinds of things do they do in the snow?**
Cooper and Bella build a snowman and go sleigh riding in the snow.

🐾 **What color is Cooper's sled?**
Cooper's sled is bright green.

🐾 **What happens with the weather when they begin sledding on the big hill?**
It starts to snow when they begin sledding on the big hill.

🐾 **What does Cooper put on his eyes when it starts to snow?**
He puts goggles on his eyes when it starts to snow so that he can see better and protect his eyes.

🐾 **What happens when they go to the bottom of the hill?**
When they go to the bottom of the hill, the snow is falling so quickly that they can hardly see. Everything looks white.

🐾 **Why do Cooper and Bella sit and wait in the snow?**
Cooper and Bella wait in the snow because they don't know how to get back home. They are lost. Nothing looks the same in the snow, and they are waiting to see if the snow will stop.

Cooper and Me™
and the Winter Adventure!

Learning Together

🐾 **Why do Cooper and Bella begin barking as loud as they can?**
Cooper and Bella begin barking as loud as they can hoping someone will hear them and come find them.

🐾 **When they hear another bark, what do they do?**
When they hear another bark, they walk toward the barking to see who it is.

🐾 **Who is the one barking that leads them home?**
Trooper, their friend, is the one barking. He leads them home.

🐾 **How do you think they feel when they don't know where they are?**
Open discussion. Talk about the situation. It is cold and getting dark, and they are lost. Discuss how this would make you feel.

🐾 **Have you ever felt scared when you thought you were lost?**
Open discussion.

🐾 **What kinds of things could they have done before they went sledding to help them in case they got lost?**
If Cooper and Bella had told someone where they were going before they headed out, then others would have known where to look for them. Sharing your plans with others can help you be more prepared and safe.

🐾 **What are some things you should know about yourself that will help you if you get lost?**
In case you get lost, you should always know your full name (first and last name), your parents' full names, your address, and your phone number.